a bear, a bee, and a honey tree

words by
Daniel Bernstrom

art by
Brandon James Scott

Hippo Park

a bear

a bee

a honey tree

a honey bee

a bear

a hungry bear

a honey bear

a hungry bear

a busy bee

a bear
and a bee
in a honey tree

a busy bee

a busy bear

a sneaky
busy honey bear

a fretful bee

a paw in tree

a very
angry
fuzzy bee

a grumbling bee
a rumbling tree

a million fuzzy buzzing bees

a tumbling bear

a swarm of bees

a running bear

a patch of weeds

a million bees up in the air

a searching bee

a hiding bear

a million busy
buzzing bees

returning to
their honey tree

and somewhere...

a hungry
grumbly
honey bear

To my mentor Emily Jenkins and
the Southwest Minnesota Arts Council
for funding the creation of this work

-D. B.

For all the bears in the world who don't give up

-B. J. S.

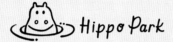 Hippo Park

An imprint of Astra Books for Young Readers,
a division of Astra Publishing House
astrapublishinghouse.com
Printed in China
ISBN: 978-1-6626-4008-7 (hc)
ISBN: 978-1-6626-4009-4 (eBook)
Library of Congress Control Number: 2021922642

First edition

10 9 8 7 6 5 4 3 2 1

Design by Jill Turney
The text and titles are set in Aniara.
The illustrations are rendered digitally.